The Night Before Christmas

The New Directions Pearls

César Aira, *The Literary Conference*

Jorge Luis Borges, *Everything and Nothing*

Sir Thomas Browne, *Urn Burial*

F. Scott Fitzgerald, *On Booze*

Nikolai Gogol, *The Night Before Christmas*

Federico García Lorca, *In Search of Duende*

Javier Marías, *Bad Nature, or With Elvis in Mexico*

Yukio Mishima, *Patriotism*

Victor Pelevin, *The Hall of the Singing Caryatids*

Joseph Roth, *The Leviathan*

Tennessee Williams, *Tales of Desire*

Forthcoming

Roberto Bolaño, *Antwerp*

Robert Walser, *The Walk*

The Night Before Christmas

·

NIKOLAI GOGOL

Translated by Constance Garnett

A NEW DIRECTIONS PEARL

Manufactured in the United States of America
New Directions Books are printed on acid-free paper.
First published as a Pearl (NDP1214) by New Directions in 2011
Published simultaneously in Canada by Penguin Books Canada Limited
Designed by Erik Rieselbach
Set in Albertina

Library of Congress Cataloging-in-Publication Data

Gogol, Nikolai Vasilievich, 1809–1852.
[Noch, pered Rozhdestvom. English]
The night before Christmas / Nikolai Gogol ; translated by Constance Garnett.
p. cm.
"A New Directions Pearl."
ISBN 978-0-8112-1947-1 (paperbook : acid-free paper)
1. Christmas—Russia—Fiction. I. Garnett, Constance, 1861–1946. II. Title.
PG3333.N63 2011
891.73'3—dc23

                    2011032969

10 9 8 7 6 5 4 3 2 1

New Directions Books are published for James Laughlin
by New Directions Publishing Corporation
80 Eighth Avenue, New York, NY 10011

THE NIGHT BEFORE CHRISTMAS

THE LAST DAY BEFORE CHRISTMAS HAD PASSED. A clear winter night had come; the stars peeped out; the moon rose majestically in the sky to light good people and all the world so that all might enjoy singing *kolyadki* and praising the Lord.* It was freezing harder than in the morning; but it was so still that the crunch of the snow under the boot could be heard half a mile away. Not one group of lads had appeared under the cottage windows yet; only the moon peeped in at them stealthily as though calling to the girls who were dressing up in their best to make haste and run out on the crunching snow. At that moment the smoke rose in puffs from a cottage chimney and passed like a cloud over the sky, and a witch, astride

*Among us it is the custom to sing under the window on Christmas Eve carols that are called *kolyadki*. The mistress or master or whoever is left in the house always drops into the singer's bag some sausage or bread or a copper or whatever he has plenty of. It is said that once upon a time there was a blockhead called Kolyada who was taken to be a god and that these *kolyadki* came from that. Who knows? It is not for plain folk like us to give our opinion about it. Last year Father Osip was for forbidding them to sing *kolyadki* about the farms, saying that folk were honoring Satan by doing so, though to tell the truth there is not a word about Kolyada in the *kolyadki*. They often sing about the birth of Christ, and at the end wish good health to the master, the mistress, the children, and all the household.— (*The Bee-keeper's Note.*)

a broomstick, rose up in the air together with the smoke.

If the assessor of Sorotchintsy, in his cap edged with lambskin and cut like an Uhlan's, in his dark blue great-coat lined with black astrakhan, had driven by at that moment with his three hired horses and the fiendishly plaited whip with which it is his habit to urge on his coachman, he would certainly have noticed her, for there is not a witch in the world who could elude the eyes of the Sorotchintsy assessor. He can count on his fingers how many little pigs every peasant-woman's sow has farrowed and how much linen is lying in her chest and just which of her clothes and household belongings her goodman pawns on Sunday at the tavern. But the Sorotchintsy assessor did not drive by, and, indeed, what business is it of his? He has his own district. Meanwhile, the witch rose so high in the air that she was only a little black patch gleaming up aloft. But wherever that little patch appeared, there the stars one after another vanished. Soon the witch had gathered a whole sleeveful of them. Three or four were still shining. All at once from the opposite side another little patch appeared, grew larger, began to lengthen out, and was no longer a little patch. A short-sighted man would never have made out what it was, even if he had put the wheels of the Commissar's chaise on his nose by way of spectacles. At first it looked like a regular German:* the narrow little face,

*Among us everyone is called a German who comes from a foreign country; even if he is a Frenchman, a Hungarian, or a Swede—he is still a German.

continually twisting and turning and sniffing at everything, ended in a little round heel, like our pigs' snouts; the legs were so thin, that if the mayor of Yareskovo had had legs like that, he would certainly have broken them in the first Cossack dance. But behind he was for all the world a district attorney in uniform, for he had a tail as long and pointed as the uniform coat-tails are nowadays. It was only from the goat-beard under his chin, from the little horns sticking upon his forehead, and from his being no whiter than a chimney-sweep, that one could tell that he was not a German or a district attorney, but simply the devil, who had one last night left him to wander about the wide world and teach good folk to sin. On the morrow when the first bells rang for matins, he would run with his tail between his legs straight off to his lair.

Meanwhile the devil stole silently up to the moon and stretched his hand out to seize it, but drew it back quickly as though he were scorched, sucked his fingers and danced about, then ran up from the other side and again skipped away and drew back his hand. But in spite of all his failures the sly devil did not give up his tricks. Running up, he suddenly seized the moon with both hands; grimacing and blowing, he kept flinging it from one hand to the other, like a peasant who has picked up an ember for his pipe with bare fingers; at last, he hurriedly put it in his pocket and ran on as though nothing had happened.

No one in Dikanka noticed that the devil had stolen the

moon. It is true the district clerk, coming out of the tavern on all fours, saw the moon for no reason whatever dancing in the sky, and he swore he had to the whole village; but people shook their heads and even made fun of him. But what motive led the devil to this lawless act? Why, this was how it was; he knew that the rich Cossack, Tchub, had been invited by the sacristan to a supper of frumenty at which a kinsman of the sacristan's, who had come from the bishop's choir, wore a dark blue coat and could take the very lowest bass-note, the mayor, the Cossack Sverbyguz and some others were to be present, and at which besides the Christmas frumenty there were to be mulled vodka, saffron vodka and good things of all sorts. And meanwhile his daughter, the greatest beauty in the village, was left at home, and there was no doubt that the blacksmith, a very strong and fine young fellow, would pay her a visit, and him the devil hated more than Father Kondrat's sermons. In his spare time the blacksmith had taken up painting and was reckoned the finest artist in the whole countryside. Even the Cossack officer L——ko, who was still strong and hearty in those days, sent for him to Poltava expressly to paint a paling fence round his house. All the bowls from which the Cossacks of Dikanka supped their beetroot soup had been painted by the blacksmith. He was a God-fearing man and often painted ikons of the saints: even now you may find his Luke the Evangelist in the church of T. But the triumph of his art was a picture painted on the church wall in the chapel on the right. In it he depicted St. Peter on the Day of Judgment with the keys in his hand driving the Evil Spirit out of hell: the frightened devil was running in all directions, foreseeing his doom, while the sinners, who had been imprisoned before, were chasing him and striking him with whips, blocks of wood and anything they could get hold of. While the artist was working at this picture and painting it on a big wooden board, the devil did all he could to hinder him; he gave him a nudge on the arm, unseen, blew some ashes from the forge in the smithy and scattered them on the picture; but, in spite of it all, the work was finished, the picture was brought into the church and put on the wall of the side-chapel, and from that day the devil has sworn to revenge himself on the blacksmith.

He had only one night left to wander upon earth; but he was looking for some means of venting his wrath on the blacksmith that night. And that was why he made up his mind to steal the moon, reckoning that old Tchub was lazy and slow to move, and the sacristan's cottage a good long step away: the road passed by cross paths beside the mills and the graveyard and went round a ravine. On a moonlit night mulled vodka and saffron vodka might have tempted Tchub; but in such darkness it was doubtful whether anyone could drag him from the stove and bring him out of the cottage. And the blacksmith, who had for a long time been on bad terms with him, would on no account have ventured, strong as he was, to visit the daughter when the father was at home.

And so, as soon as the devil had hidden the moon in his pocket, it was at once so dark all over the world that not everyone could have found the way to the tavern, let alone to the sacristan's. The witch gave a shriek when she suddenly found herself in darkness. Then the devil running up, all bows and smiles, put his arm round her and began whispering in her ear the sort of thing that is usually whispered to all the female sex. Things are queerly arranged in our world! All who live in it are always trying to outdo and imitate one another. In the old days the judge and the police-captain were the only ones in Mirgorod who used to wear cloth overcoats lined with sheepskin in the winter, while all the minor officials wore plain sheepskin; but nowadays the assessor and the chamberlain have managed to get themselves new cloth greatcoats lined with astrakhan. The year before last the treasury clerk and the district clerk bought dark blue duck at sixty kopecks a yard. The sexton has got himself nankeen trousers for the summer and a striped waistcoat of camel's hair. In fact everyone tries to be somebody! When will folks give up being vain! I am ready to bet that many would be surprised to see the devil carrying on in that way. What is most annoying is that, no doubt, he fancies himself a handsome fellow, though his figure is a shameful sight. With a face, as Foma Grigoryevitch used to say, the abomination of abominations, yet even he plays the gallant! But in the sky and under the sky it was growing so dark that there was no seeing what followed between them.

"So you have not been to see the sacristan in his new cottage, mate?" said the Cossack Tchub, coming out at his door to a tall lean peasant in a short sheepskin, whose stubby beard showed that for at least a fortnight it had not been touched by the broken piece of scythe with which for lack of a razor peasants usually shave their beards. "There will be a fine drinking-party there tonight!" Tchub went on, grinning as he spoke. "If only we are not late!"

Hereupon Tchub set straight the belt that closely girt his sheepskin, pulled his cap more firmly on his head, and gripped his whip, the terror and the menace of tiresome dogs; but glancing upward, he stopped. "What the devil! Look! look, Panas ... !"

"What?" articulated his friend, and he too turned his face upward.

"What, indeed! There is no moon!"

"What a nuisance! There really is no moon."

"That's just it, there isn't!" Tchub brought out, with some annoyance at his friend's imperturbable indifference. "You don't care, I'll be bound."

"Well, what can I do about it?"

"Some devil," Tchub went on, wiping his moustaches with his sleeve, "must needs go and meddle—may he

9

never have a glass of vodka to drink in the mornings, the dog! Upon my word, it's as though to mock us.... As I sat indoors I looked out of the window and the night was lovely! It was light, the snow was sparkling in the moonlight; you could see everything as though it were day. And here before I'm out of the door, you can't see your hand before your face! May he break his teeth on a crust of buckwheat bread!"

Tchub went on grumbling and scolding for a long while, and at the same time he was hesitating what to decide. He had a desperate longing to gossip over all sorts of nonsense at the sacristan's, where no doubt the mayor was already sitting, as well as the bass choir-singer, and Mikita, the tar-dealer, who used to come once a fortnight on his way to Poltava, and who cracked such jokes that all the village worthies held their sides with laughing. Already in his mind's eye Tchub saw the mulled vodka on the table. All this was alluring, it is true, but the darkness of the night recalled the charms of laziness, so dear to every Cossack. How nice it would be now to lie on the ovenstep with his legs tucked under him, quietly smoking his pipe and listening through a luxurious drowsiness to the songs and carols of the lighthearted lads and lasses who gathered in groups under the windows! He would undoubtedly have decided on the latter course had he been alone; but for the two together, it was not so dreary and terrible to go through the dark night; besides he did not care to seem sluggish and cowardly to others. When he had finished scolding he turned again to his friend.

"So there is no moon, mate?"

"No!"

"It's strange really! Let me have a pinch of snuff! You have splendid snuff, mate! Where do you get it?"

"Splendid! Devil a bit of it!" answered the friend, shutting the birchbark snuffbox with patterns pricked out upon it. "It wouldn't make an old hen sneeze!"

"I remember," Tchub still went on, "the innkeeper, Zuzulya, once brought me some snuff from Nyezhin. Ah, that was snuff! it was good snuff! So how is it to be, mate? It's dark, you know!"

"So maybe we'll stay at home," his friend brought out, taking hold of the door-handle.

If his friend had not said that, Tchub would certainly have made up his mind to stay at home; but now something seemed egging him on to oppose it. "No, mate, let us go! It won't do, we must go!"

Even as he was saying it, he was vexed with himself that he had said it. He very much disliked turning out on such a night, but it was a comfort to him that he was acting on his own decision and not following advice.

His friend looked round and scratched his shoulders with the handle of his whip, without the slightest sign of vexation on his face, like a man to whom it is a matter of complete indifference whether he sits at home or goes out—and the two friends set off on their road.

* * *

Now let us see what Tchub's daughter, the beauty, was doing all by herself. Before Oksana was seventeen, people were talking about nothing but her in almost the whole world, both on this side of Dikanka and on the other side of Dikanka. The lads were all at one in declaring that there never had been and never would be a finer girl in the village. Oksana heard and knew all that was said about her and, like a beauty, was full of caprices. If, instead of a checked skirt and an apron, she had been dressed as a lady, she could never have kept a servant. The lads ran after her in crowds, but, losing patience, by degrees forsook the willful beauty, and turned to others who were not so spoilt. Only the blacksmith was persistent and would not abandon his courtship, although he was treated not a whit better than the rest. When her father went out. Oksana spent a long while yet dressing herself in her best and preening before a little looking-glass in a pewter frame; she could not tear herself away from admiring herself.

"What put it into folks' heads to spread it abroad that I am pretty?" she said, as it were without thinking, simply to talk to herself about something. "Folks lie, I am not pretty at all!"

But the fresh living face reflected in the looking-glass, in its childish youthfulness, with its sparkling black eyes and inexpressibly charming smile that stirred the soul, at once proved the contrary.

"Can my black eyebrows and my eyes," the beauty went on, still holding the mirror, "be so beautiful that there are none like them in the world? What is there pretty in that turned-up nose, and in the cheeks and the lips? Is my black hair pretty? Ough, my curls might frighten one in the evening, they twist and twine round my head like long snakes! I see now that I am not pretty at all!" And, moving the looking-glass a little further away, she cried out: "No, I am pretty! Ah, how pretty! Wonderful! What a joy I shall be to the man whose wife I become! How my husband will admire me! He'll be wild with joy. He will kiss me to death!"

"Wonderful girl!" whispered the blacksmith, coming in softly. "And hasn't she a little conceit! She's been standing looking in the mirror for an hour and can't tear herself away, and praising herself aloud, too!"

"Yes, lads, I am a match for you? Just look at me!" the pretty coquette went on: "how gracefully I step; my shift is embroidered with red silk. And the ribbons on my head! You will never see richer braid! My father bought me all this that the finest young man in the world may marry me." And, laughing, she turned around and saw the blacksmith....

She uttered a shriek and stood still, coldly facing him.

The blacksmith's hands dropped helplessly to his sides.

It is hard to describe what the dark face of the lovely girl expressed. There was sternness in it, and through the sternness a sort of defiance of the embarrassed blacksmith, and at the same time a hardly perceptible flush of vexation delicately suffused her face; and all this was so mingled and so indescribably pretty that to give her a million kisses was the best thing that could have been done at the moment.

"Why have you come here?" was how Oksana began. "Do you want me to shove you out of the door with a spade? You are all very clever at coming to see us. You sniff out in a minute when there are no fathers in the house. Oh, I know you! Well, is my chest ready?"

"It will be ready, my little heart, it will be ready after Christmas. If only you knew how I have worked at it; for two nights I didn't leave the smithy. But, there, no priest's wife will have a chest like it. The iron I bound it with is better than what I put on the officer's chariot, when I worked at Poltava. And how it will be painted! You won't find one like it if you wander over the whole neighborhood with your little white feet! Red and blue flowers will be scattered over the whole ground. It will glow like fire. Don't be angry with me! Allow me at least to speak to you, to look at you!"

"Who's forbidding you? Speak and look!"

Hereupon she sat down on the bench, glanced again at the looking-glass, and began arranging her hair. She looked at her neck, at her shift, embroidered in red silk, and a subtle feeling of complacency could be read on her lips and fresh cheeks, and was reflected in her eyes.

"Allow me to sit beside you," said the blacksmith.

"Sit down," said Oksana, with the same emotion still perceptible on her lips and in her gratified eyes.

"Wonderful, lovely Oksana, allow me to kiss you!" ventured the blacksmith, growing bolder, and he drew her toward him with the intention of snatching a kiss. But Oksana turned away her cheek, which had been exceeding close to the blacksmith's lips, and pushed him away.

"What more do you want? When there's honey he must have a spoonful! Go away, your hands are harder than iron. And you smell of smoke. I believe you have smeared me all over with your soot."

Then she picked up the looking-glass and began preening again.

"She does not love me!" the blacksmith thought to himself, hanging his head. "It's all play to her while I stand before her like a fool and cannot take my eyes off her. And I should like to stand before her always and never to take my eyes off her! Wonderful girl! What would I not give to know what is in her heart, and whom she loves. But no, she cares for nobody. She is admiring herself; she is tormenting poor me, while I am so sad that everything is darkness to me. I love her as no man in the world ever has loved or ever will."

"Is it true that your mother's a witch?" Oksana brought out, and she laughed. And the blacksmith felt that everything within him was laughing. That laugh echoed as it were at once in his heart and in his softly thrilling veins, and for all that his soul was vexed that he had not the right to kiss that sweetly laughing face.

"What care I for mother? You are father and mother to me and all that is precious in the world. If the Tsar summoned me and said: 'Smith Vakula, ask me for all that is best in my kingdom, I will give you anything. I will bid them make you a golden forge and you shall work with silver hammers.' 'I don't care,' I should say to the Tsar, 'for precious stones or a golden forge nor for all your kingdom: give me rather my Oksana.'"

"You see, what a fellow you are! Only my father's no fool either. You'll see that, when he doesn't marry your mother!" Oksana said, smiling slyly. "But the girls are not here.... What's the meaning of it? We ought to have been singing long ago, I am getting tired of waiting."

"Let them stay away, my beauty!"

"I should hope not! I expect the lads will come with them. And then there will be dances. I can fancy what funny stories they will tell!"

"So you'll be merry with them?"

"Yes, merrier than with you. Ah! someone knocked; I expect it is the girls and the lads."

"What's the use of my staying longer?" the blacksmith said to himself. "She is jeering at me. I am no more to her than an old rusty horseshoe. But if that's so, anyway I won't let another man laugh at me. If only I see for certain that she likes someone better than me, I'll teach him to keep off...."

A knock at the door and a cry of "Open!" ringing out sharply in the frost interrupted his reflections.

"Stay, I'll open the door," said the blacksmith, and he went out intending in his vexation to break the ribs of anyone who might be there.

The frost grew sharper, and up aloft it turned so cold that the devil kept hopping from one hoof to the other and blowing into his fists, trying to warm his frozen hands. And indeed it is small wonder that he should be cold, being used day after day to knocking about in hell, where, as we all know, it is not so cold as it is with us in winter, and where, putting on his cap and standing before the hearth, like a real cook, he fries sinners with as much satisfaction as a peasant-woman fries a sausage at Christmas.

The witch herself felt that it was cold, although she was warmly clad; and so, throwing her arms upward, she stood with one foot out, and putting herself into the attitude of a man flying along on skates, without moving a single muscle, she dropped through the air, as though on an ice-slope, and straight into her chimney.

The devil set off after her in the same way. But as the creature is nimbler than any dandy in stockings, there is no wonder that he reached the top of the chimney almost on the neck of his mistress, and both found themselves in a roomy oven among the pots.

The witch stealthily moved back the oven door to see whether her son, Vakula, had invited visitors to the cottage; but seeing that there was no one, except the sacks that lay in the middle of the floor, she crept out of the oven, flung off her warm pelisse, set herself to rights, and no one could have told that she had been riding on a broom the minute before.

Vakula's mother was not more than forty years old. She was neither handsome nor ugly. Indeed, it is hard to be handsome at such an age. However, she was so clever at alluring even the steadiest Cossacks (who, it may not be amiss to observe, do not care much about beauty) that the mayor and the sacristan, Osip Nikiforovitch (if his wife were not at home, of course), and the Cossack, Korny Tchub, and the Cossack, Kassian Sverbyguz, were all dancing attendance on her. And it must be said to her credit that she was very skillful in managing them: not one of them dreamed that he had a rival. If a God-fearing peasant or a gentleman (as the Cossacks call themselves) wearing a cape with a hood went to church on Sunday or, if the weather was bad, to the tavern, how could he fail to look in on Soloha, eat curd dumplings with sour cream, and gossip in the warm cottage with its chatty and agreeable mistress? And the Cossack would purposely go a long way round before reaching the tavern, and would call that "looking in on his way." And when Soloha went to church on a holiday, dressed in a bright-checked *plahta* with a cotton *zapaska*, and above it a dark blue overskirt on the back of which gold flourishes were embroidered, and took up her stand close to the right side of the choir, the sacristan would be sure to begin coughing and unconsciously screw up his eyes in her direction; the mayor would smooth his moustaches, begin twisting the curl behind his ear, and say to the man standing next to him: "Ah, a nice woman, a devil of a woman!" Soloha would bow to each one of them, and each one would think that she was bowing to him alone.

But anyone fond of meddling in other people's business would notice at once that Soloha was most gracious to the Cossack Tchub. Tchub was a widower. Eight stacks of wheat always stood before his cottage. Two pairs of stalwart oxen poked their heads out of the thatched barn by the roadside and mooed every time they saw their crony, the cow, or their uncle, the stout bull, pass. A bearded billy-goat used to clamber onto the very roof, from which he would bleat in a harsh voice like the police-captain's, taunting the turkeys when they came out into the yard, and turning his back when he saw his enemies, the boys, who used to jeer at his beard. In Tchub's trunks there was plenty of linen and many full coats and old-fashioned over-dresses with gold lace on them; his wife had been fond of fine clothes. In his vegetable patch, besides poppies, cabbages, and sunflowers, two beds were sown every year with tobacco. Soloha thought that it would not be amiss to join all this to her own farm, and, already reckoning in what good order it would be when it passed into her hands, she felt doubly well-disposed to old Tchub. And to prevent her son Vakula from courting Tchub's daughter and succeeding in getting possession of it all himself (then he would very likely not let her interfere in anything), she had recourse to the common maneuver of all dames of forty—that is, setting Tchub at loggerheads with the blacksmith as often as she could.* Possibly these sly tricks and subtlety were the reason that the old women were beginning here and there, particularly when they had drunk a drop too much at some merry gathering, to say that Soloha was certainly a witch, that the lad Kizyakolupenko had seen a tail on her back no bigger than a peasant-woman's distaff; that, no longer ago than the Thursday before last, she had run across the road in the form of a black cat; that on one occasion a sow had run up to the priest's wife, had crowed like a cock, put Father Kondrat's cap on her head, and run away again.…

It happened that just when the old women were talking about this, a cowherd, Tymish Korostyavy, came up. He did not fail to tell them how in the summer, just before St. Peter's Fast, when he had lain down to sleep in the stable, putting some straw under his head, he saw with his own eyes a witch, with her hair down, in nothing but her shift,

---

*Had her son married Tchub's daughter, she could not by the rules of the Russian Church have married Tchub.— (*Translator's Note.*)

begin milking the cows, and he could not stir he was so spellbound, and she had smeared his lips with something so nasty that he was spitting the whole day afterwards. But all that was somewhat doubtful, for the only one who can see a witch is the assessor of Sorotchintsy. And so all the notable Cossacks waved their hands impatiently when they heard such tales. "They are lying, the bitches!" was their usual answer.

After she had crept out of the stove and set herself to rights, Soloha, like a good housewife, began tidying up and putting everything in its place; but she did not touch the sacks. "Vakula brought those in, let him take them out himself!" she thought. Meanwhile the devil, who had chanced to turn round just as he was flying into the chimney, had caught sight of Tchub arm-in-arm with his neighbor already a long way from home. Instantly he flew out of the chimney, cut across their road, and began flinging up heaps of frozen snow in all directions. A blizzard sprang up. All was whiteness in the air. The snow zigzagged like network behind and in front and threatened to plaster up the eyes, the mouth, and the ears of the friends. And the devil flew back to the chimney again in the firm conviction that Tchub would go back home with his neighbor, would find the blacksmith there and probably give him such a dressing-down that it would be a long time before he would be able to handle a brush and paint offensive caricatures.

* * *

As a matter of fact, as soon as the blizzard began and the wind blew straight in their faces, Tchub expressed his regret, and pulling his hood further down on his head showered abuse on himself, the devil, and his friend. His annoyance was feigned, however. Tchub was really glad of the snowstorm. They had still eight times as far to go as they had gone already before they would reach the sacristan's. They turned round. The wind blew on the back of their heads, but they could see nothing through the whirling snow.

"Stay, mate! I fancy we are going wrong," said Tchub, after walking on a little. "I do not see a single cottage. Oh, what a snowstorm! You go a little that way, mate, and see whether you find the road, and meanwhile I'll look this way. It was the foul fiend put it into my head to go trudging out in such a storm! Don't forget to shout when you find the road. Oh what a heap of snow Satan has driven into my eyes!"

The road was not to be seen, however. Tchub's friend, turning off, wandered up and down in his long boots, and at last came straight upon the tavern. This lucky find so cheered him that he forgot everything and, shaking the snow off, walked straight in, not worrying himself in the least about the friend he had left on the road. Meanwhile Tchub fancied that he had found the road. Standing still, he fell to shouting at the top of his voice, but, seeing that his friend did not appear, he made up his mind to go on alone. After walking on a little he saw his own cottage. Snowdrifts lay all about it and on the roof. Clapping his frozen hands together, he began knocking at the door and shouting peremptorily to his daughter to open it.

"What do you want here?" the blacksmith called grimly, as he came out.

Tchub, recognizing the blacksmith's voice, stepped back a little. "Ah, no, it's not my cottage," he said to himself. "The blacksmith doesn't come into my cottage. Though, as I come to look well, it is not the blacksmith's either. Whose cottage can it be? I know! I didn't recognize it! It's where lame Levtchenko lives, who has lately married a young wife. His is the only cottage that is like mine. I did think it was a little queer that I had reached home so soon. But Levtchenko is at the sacristan's now, I know that. Why is the blacksmith here ...? Ah, a-ha! he comes to see his young wife. So that's it! Good ...! Now I understand it all."

"Who are you and what are you hanging about at people's doors for?" said the blacksmith more grimly than before, coming closer to him.

"No, I am not going to tell him who I am," thought Tchub. "He'll give me a good drubbing, I shouldn't wonder, the damned brute." And, disguising his voice, he answered: "It's I, good man! I have come for your diversion to sing carols under your windows."

"Go to the devil with your carols!" Vakula shouted angrily. "Why are you standing there? Do you hear! Be off with you."

Tchub already had that prudent intention; but it annoyed him to be forced to obey the blacksmith's orders. It seemed as though some evil spirit nudged his arm and compelled him to say something contradictory. "Why are you bawling like that?" he said in the same voice. "I want to sing carols and that's enough!"

"A-ha! I see words aren't enough for you!" And upon that Tchub felt a very painful blow on his shoulder.

"So I see you are beginning to fight now!" he said, stepping back a little.

"Be off, be off!" shouted the blacksmith, giving Tchub another shove.

"Well, you are!" said Tchub in a voice that betrayed pain, annoyance, and timidity. "You are fighting in earnest, I see, and hitting pretty hard, too."

"Be off, be off!" shouted the blacksmith, and slammed the door.

"Look, how he swaggered!" said Tchub when he was left alone in the road. "Just try going near him! What a fellow! He's a somebody! Do you suppose I won't have the law of you? No, my dear lad, I am going straight to the Commissar. I'll teach you! I don't care if you are a blacksmith and a painter. But I must look at my back and shoulders; I believe they are black and blue. The devil's son must have hit hard. It's a pity that it is cold, and I don't want to take off my pelisse. You wait, you fiend of a blacksmith; may the devil give you a drubbing and your smithy, too; I'll make you dance! Ah, the damned rascal! But, I say, he is not at home, now. I expect Soloha is all alone. H'm … it's not far off, I might go! It's such weather now that no one will come in on us. There's no saying what may happen.… Oh dear, how hard that damned blacksmith did whack!"

Here Tchub, rubbing his back, set off in a different direction. The agreeable possibilities awaiting him in a tryst with Soloha took off the pain a little and made him insensible even to the frost, the crackling of which could be heard on all the roads in spite of the howling of the storm. At moments a look of mawkish sweetness came into his face, though the blizzard soaped his beard and mustaches with snow more briskly than any barber who tyrannically holds his victim by the nose. But if everything had not been hidden by the crisscross of the snow, Tchub might have been seen long afterward stopping and rubbing his back as he brought out: "The damned blacksmith did whack hard!" and then going on his way again.

While the nimble dandy with the tail and goat-beard was flying out of the chimney and back again into the chimney, the pouch that hung on a shoulder-belt at his side and in which he had put the stolen moon chanced to catch on something in the stove and came open—and the moon took advantage of this accident to fly up through the chimney of Soloha's cottage and to float smoothly through the sky. Everything was flooded with light. It was as though there had been no snowstorm. The snow sparkled, a broad silvery plain, studded with crystal stars. The frost seemed less cold. Groups of lads and girls appeared with sacks. Songs rang out, and under almost every cottage window were crowds of carol-singers.

How wonderful is the light of the moon! It is hard to put into words how pleasant it is on such a night to mingle in a group of singing, laughing girls and among lads ready for every jest and sport which the gaily smiling night can suggest. It is warm under the thick pelisse; the cheeks glow brighter than ever from the frost, and Old Sly himself prompts to mischief.

Groups of girls with sacks burst into Tchub's cottage and gathered round Oksana. The blacksmith was deafened by the shouts, the laughter, the stories. They vied with one another in telling the beauty some bit of news, in emptying their sacks and boasting of the little loaves, the sausages and curd dumplings of which they had already gathered a fair harvest from their singing. Oksana seemed to be highly pleased and delighted, she chatted first with one and then with another and laughed without ceasing.

With what envy and vexation the blacksmith looked at this gaiety, and this time he cursed the carol-singing, though he was passionately fond of it himself.

"Ah, Odarka!" said the light-hearted beauty, turning to one of the girls, "you have some new slippers. Ah, how pretty! And with gold on them! It's nice for you, Odarka, you have a man who will buy you anything, but I have no one to get me such splendid slippers."

"Don't grieve, my precious Oksana!" put in the blacksmith. "I will get you slippers such as not many a lady wears."

"You!" said Oksana, with a rapid and haughty glance at him. "I should like to know where you'll get hold of slippers such as I could put on my feet. Perhaps you will bring me the very ones the Tsaritsa wears?"

"You see the sort she wants!" cried the crowd of girls, laughing.

"Yes!" the beauty went on proudly, "all of you be my witnesses: if the blacksmith Vakula brings me the very slippers the Tsaritsa wears, here's my word on it, I'll marry him that very day."

The girls carried off the capricious beauty with them.

"Laugh away! laugh away!" thought the blacksmith as he followed them out. "I laugh at myself! I wonder and can't think what I have done with my senses! She does not love me—well, let her go! As though there were no one in the world but Oksana. Thank God, there are lots of fine girls besides her in the village. And what is Oksana? She'll never make a good housewife; the only thing she is good at is dressing up. No, it's enough! It's time I gave up playing the fool!"

But at the very time when the blacksmith was making up his mind to be resolute, some evil spirit set floating before him the laughing image of Oksana saying mockingly, "Get me the Tsaritsa's slippers, blacksmith, and I will marry you!" Everything within him was stirred and he could think of nothing but Oksana.

The crowds of carol-singers, the lads in one party and the girls in another, hurried from one street to the next. But the blacksmith went on and saw nothing, and took no part in the merrymaking which he had once loved more than anything.

Meanwhile the devil was making love in earnest at Soloha's: kissed her hand with the same airs and graces as the assessor does the priest's daughter's, put his hand on his heart, sighed, and said bluntly that, if she would not consent to gratify his passion and reward his devotion in the usual way, he was ready for anything: would fling himself in the water and let his soul go straight to hell. Soloha was not so cruel; besides, the devil as we know was alone with her. She was fond of seeing a crowd hanging about her and was rarely without company. That evening, however, she was expecting to spend alone, because all the noteworthy inhabitants of the village had been invited to keep Christmas Eve at the sacristan's. But it turned out otherwise: the devil had only just urged his suit, when suddenly they heard a knock and the voice of the stalwart mayor. Soloha ran to open the door, while the nimble devil crept into a sack that was lying on the floor.

The mayor, after shaking the snow off his cap and drinking a glass of vodka from Soloha's hand, told her that he had not gone to the sacristan's because it had begun to snow; and, seeing a light in her cottage, had dropped in, meaning to spend the evening with her.

The mayor had hardly had time to say this when they heard a knock at the door and the voice of the sacristan: "Hide me somewhere," whispered the mayor. "I don't want to meet the sacristan now."

Soloha thought for some time where to hide so bulky a visitor; at last she selected the biggest coal-sack. She shot the coal out into a barrel, and the stalwart mayor, mustaches, head, pelisse, and all, crept into the sack.

The sacristan walked in, clearing his throat and rubbing his hands, and told her that no one had come to his party and that he was heartily glad of this opportunity to enjoy a visit to her and was not afraid of the snowstorm. Then he went closer to her and, with a cough and a smirk, touched her plump bare arm with his long fingers and said with an air expressive both of slyness and satisfaction: "And what have you here, magnificent Soloha?" and saying this he stepped back a little.

"What do you mean? My arm, Osip Nikiforovitch!" answered Soloha.

"H'm! your arm! He—he—he!" cried the sacristan, highly delighted with his opening. And he paced up and down the room.

"And what have you here, incomparable Soloha …?" he said with the same air, going up to her again, lightly touching her neck and skipping back again in the same way.

"As though you don't see, Osip Nikiforovitch!" answered Soloha; "my neck and my necklace on my neck."

"H'm! A necklace on your neck! He—he—he!" and the sacristan walked again up and down the room, rubbing his hands.

"And what have you here, incomparable Soloha …?" There's no telling what the sacristan (a carnal-minded man) might have touched next with his long fingers, when suddenly they heard a knock at the door and the voice of the Cossack Tchub.

"Oh dear, someone who's not wanted!" cried the sacristan in alarm. "What now if I am caught here, a person of my position …! It will come to Father Kondrat's ears…."

But the sacristan's apprehensions were really of a different nature; he was more afraid that his doings might come to the knowledge of his better half, whose terrible hand had already turned his thick mane into a very scanty one. "For God's sake, virtuous Soloha!" he said, trembling all over, "your lovingkindness, as it says in the Gospel of St. Luke, chapter thirt … thirt … What a knocking, oh dear, what a knocking! Ough, hide me somewhere!"

Soloha turned the coal out of another sack, and the sacristan, whose proportions were not too ample, crept into it and settled at the very bottom, so that another half-sack of coal might have been put in on the top of him.

"Good evening, Soloha!" said Tchub, as he came into the cottage. "Maybe you didn't expect me, eh? You didn't, did you? Perhaps I am in the way ...?" Tchub went on with a good-humored and significant expression on his face, which betrayed that his slow-moving mind was at work and preparing to utter some sarcastic and amusing jest.

"Maybe you had some entertaining companion here ...! Maybe you have someone in hiding already? Eh?" And enchanted by this observation of his, Tchub laughed, inwardly triumphant at being the only man who enjoyed Soloha's favor. "Come, Soloha, let me have a drink of vodka now. I believe my throat's frozen stiff with this damned frost. God has sent us weather for Christmas Eve! How it has come on, do you hear, Soloha, how it has come on ...? Ah, my hands are stiff, I can't unbutton my sheepskin! How the storm has come on...."

"Open the door!" a voice rang out in the street accompanied by a thump on the door.

"Someone is knocking," said Tchub, standing still.

"Open!" the shout rang out louder still.

"It's the blacksmith!" cried Tchub, catching up his pelisse. "I say, Soloha, put me where you like; for nothing in the world will I show myself to that damned brute. May he have a pimple as big as a haycock under each of his eyes, the devil's son!"

Soloha, herself alarmed, flew about like one distraught

and, forgetting what she was doing, signed to Tchub to creep into the very sack in which the sacristan was already sitting. The poor sacristan dared not betray his pain by a cough or a groan when the heavy Cossack sat down almost on his head and put a frozen boot on each side of his face.

The blacksmith walked in, not saying a word or removing his cap, and almost fell down on the bench. It could be seen that he was in a very bad humor.

At the very moment when Soloha was shutting the door after him, someone knocked at the door again. This was the Cossack Sverbyguz. He could not be hidden in the sack, because no sack big enough could he found anywhere. He was more corpulent than the mayor and taller than Tchub's neighbor Panas. And so Soloha led him into the kitchen-garden to hear from him there all that he had to tell her.

The blacksmith looked absentmindedly at the corners of his cottage, listening from time to time to the voices of the carol-singers floating far away through the village. At last his eyes rested on the sacks. "Why are those sacks lying there? They ought to have been cleared away long ago. This foolish love has turned me quite silly. Tomorrow's Christmas and rubbish of all sorts is still lying about the cottage. I'll carry them to the smithy!"

Hereupon the blacksmith stooped down to the huge sacks, tied them up more tightly, and prepared to hoist them on his shoulders. But it was evident that his thoughts were straying, God knows where; or he would have heard how Tchub gasped when the hair of his head was twisted in the string that tied the sack and the stalwart mayor began hiccuping quite distinctly.

"Can nothing drive that wretched Oksana out of my head?" the blacksmith was saying. "I don't want to think about her; but I keep thinking and thinking and, as luck will have it, of her and nothing else. How is it that thoughts creep into the mind against the will? The devil! the sacks seem to have grown heavier than they were! Something besides coal must have been put into them. I am a fool! I forget that now everything seems heavier to me. In the old days I could bend and unbend again a copper coin or a horseshoe with one hand, and now I can't lift sacks of coal. I shall be blown over by the wind next.... No!" he cried, pulling himself together after a pause, "I am not a weak woman! I won't let anyone make a mock of me! If there were ten such sacks, I would lift them all." And he briskly hoisted on his shoulders the sacks which two stalwart men could not have carried. "I'll take this one too," he went on, picking up the little one at the bottom of which the devil lay curled up. "I believe I put my tools in this one." Saying this he went out of the hut whistling the song: "I can't be bothered with a wife."

The singing, laughter, and shouts sounded louder and louder in the streets. The crowds of jostling people were reinforced by newcomers from neighboring villages. The lads were full of mischief and mad pranks. Often among the carols some gay song was heard which one of the young Cossacks had made up on the spot. All at once one of the crowd would let out a begging New Year's song instead of a carol and bawl at the top of his voice:

> "Christmas faring!
> Be not sparing!
> A tart or pie, please!
> Bowl of porridge!
> String of sausage!"

A roar of laughter rewarded the wag. Little windows were thrown up and the withered hand of an old woman (the old women, together with the sedate fathers, were the only people left indoors) was thrust out with a sausage or a piece of pie.

The lads and the girls vied with one another in holding out their sacks and catching their booty. In one place the lads, coming together from all sides, surrounded a group of girls. There was loud noise and clamor; one flung a snowball, another pulled away a sack full of all sorts of good things. In another place, the girls caught a lad, gave him a kick, and sent him flying headlong with his sack into the snow. It seemed as though they were ready to make merry the whole night through. And, as though of design, the night was so splendidly warm. And the light of the moon seemed brighter still from the glitter of the snow.

The blacksmith stood still with his sacks. He fancied he heard among the crowd of girls the voice and shrill laugh of Oksana. Every vein in his body throbbed; flinging the sacks on the ground so that the sacristan at the bottom groaned over the bruise he received, and the mayor gave a loud hiccup, he strolled with the little sack on his shoulders together with a group of lads after a crowd of girls, among whom he heard the voice of Oksana.

"Yes, it is she! She stands like a queen, her black eyes sparkling. A handsome lad is telling her something. It must be amusing, for she is laughing. But she is always laughing." As it were unconsciously, he could not say how, the blacksmith squeezed his way through the crowd and stood beside her.

"Oh, Vakula, you here! Good evening!" said the beauty, with the smile which almost drove Vakula mad. "Well, have you sung many carols? Oh, but what a little sack! And have you got the slippers that the Tsaritsa wears? Get me the slippers and I will marry you …!" And laughing she ran off with the other girls.

The blacksmith stood as though rooted to the spot. "No, I cannot bear it; it's too much for me.…" he brought out at last. "But, my God, why is she so fiendishly beautiful? Her eyes, her words, and everything, well, they scorch me, they fairly scorch me…. No, I cannot master myself. It's time to put an end to it all. Damn my soul, I'll go and drown myself in the hole in the ice and it will all be over!"

Then with a resolute step he walked on, caught up the group of girls, overtook Oksana, and said in a firm voice: "Farewell, Oksana! Find any lover you like, make a fool of whom you like; but me you will not see again in this world."

The beauty seemed amazed and would have said something, but with a wave of his hand the blacksmith ran away.

"Where are you off to, Vakula?" said the lads, seeing the blacksmith running.

"Good-bye, mates!" the blacksmith shouted in answer. "Please God we shall meet again in the other world, but we shall not walk together again in this. Farewell! Do not remember evil against me! Tell Father Kondrat to sing a requiem service for my sinful soul. Sinner that I am, for the sake of worldly things, I did not finish painting the candles for the ikons of the Wonder-worker and the Mother of God. All the goods which will be found in my chest are for the Church. Farewell!"

Saying this, the blacksmith fell to running again with the sack upon his back.

"He is gone crazy!" said the lads.

"A lost soul!" an old woman, who was passing, muttered devoutly. "I must go and tell them that the blacksmith has hanged himself!"

Meanwhile, after running through several streets Vakula stopped to take breath. "Where am I running?" he thought, "as though everything were over already. I'll try one way more: I'll go to the Zaporozhets, Paunchy Patsyuk;* they say he knows all the devils and can do anything he likes. I'll go to him, for my soul is lost anyway!"

At that the devil, who had lain for a long while without moving, skipped for joy in the sack; but the blacksmith, fancying that he had somehow twitched the sack with his hand and caused the movement himself, gave the sack a punch with his stalwart fist and, shaking it on his shoulders, set off to Paunchy Patsyuk.

This Paunchy Patsyuk certainly at one time had been a Zaporozhets; but no one knew whether he had been turned out of the camp or whether he had run away from Zaporozhye of his own accord.

For a long time, ten years or perhaps fifteen, he had been living in Dikanka. At first he had lived like a true Zaporozhets: he had done no work, slept three-quarters of the day, ate as much as six mowers, and drank almost a whole pailful at a time. He had somewhere to put it all, however, for though Patsyuk was not very tall he was fairly bulky in width. Moreover, the trousers he used to wear were so full that, however long a step he took, no trace of his leg was visible, and it seemed as though a wine-distiller's cask were moving down the street. Perhaps it was just this that gave rise to his nickname, Paunchy. Before many weeks had

*Zaporozhets: A Ukrainian Cossack.— (Ed.)

passed after his coming to the village, everyone had found out that he was a wizard. If anyone were ill, he called in Patsyuk at once: Patsyuk had only to whisper a few words and it was as though the ailment had been lifted off by his hand. If it happened that a hungry gentleman was choked by a fishbone, Patsyuk could punch him so skillfully on the back that the bone went the proper way without causing any harm to the gentleman's throat. Of late years he was rarely seen anywhere. The reason of that was perhaps sloth, though possibly also the fact that it was every year becoming increasingly difficult for him to pass through a doorway. People had of late been obliged to go to him if they had need of him.

Not without some timidity, the blacksmith opened the door and saw Patsyuk sitting Turkish-fashion on the floor before a little tub on which stood a bowl of dumplings. This bowl stood as though purposely on a level with his mouth. Without moving a single finger, he bent his head a little toward the bowl and sipped the soup, from time to time catching the dumplings with his teeth.

"Well," thought Vakula to himself, "this fellow's even lazier than Tchub; he eats with a spoon, anyway, while this fellow won't even lift his hand!"

Patsyuk must have been entirely engrossed with the dumplings, for he seemed to be quite unaware of the entrance of the blacksmith, who made him a very low bow as soon as he stepped on the threshold.

"I have come to ask you a favor, Patsyuk!" said Vakula, bowing again.

Fat Patsyuk lifted his head and again began swallowing dumplings.

"They say that you—no offense meant ..." the blacksmith said, taking heart, "I speak of this not by way of any insult to you—that you are a little akin to the devil."

When he had uttered these words, Vakula was alarmed, thinking that he had expressed himself too bluntly and had not sufficiently softened his language, and, expecting that Patsyuk would pick up the tub together with the bowl and fling them straight at his head, he turned aside a little and covered his face with his sleeve so that the hot dumpling soup might not spatter it. But Patsyuk looked up and again began swallowing the dumplings.

The blacksmith, reassured, made up his mind to go on. "I have come to you, Patsyuk. God give you everything, goods of all sorts in abundance and bread in proportion!" (The blacksmith would sometimes throw in a fashionable word: he had got into the way of it during his stay in Poltava when he was painting the paling-fence for the officer.) "There is nothing but ruin before me, a sinner! Nothing in the world will help! What will be, will be. I have to ask help from the devil himself. Well, Patsyuk," the blacksmith brought out, seeing his unchanged silence, "what am I to do?"

"If you need the devil, then go to the devil," answered

Patsyuk, not lifting his eyes to him, but still making away with the dumplings.

"It is for that that I have come to you," answered the blacksmith, dropping another bow to him. "I suppose that nobody in the world but you knows the way to him!"

Patsyuk answered not a word, but ate up the remaining dumplings. "Do me a kindness, good man, do not refuse me!" persisted the blacksmith, "Whether it is pork or sausage or buckwheat flour or linen, say—millet or anything else in case of need ... as is usual between good people ... we will not grudge it. Tell me at least how, for instance, to get on the road to him."

"He need not go far who has the devil on his shoulders!" Patsyuk pronounced carelessly, without changing his position.

Vakula fastened his eyes upon him as though the interpretation of those words were written on his brow. "What does he mean?" his face asked dumbly, while his mouth stood half-open ready to swallow the first word like a dumpling.

But Patsyuk was still silent.

Then Vakula noticed that there were neither dumplings nor a tub before him; but two wooden bowls were standing on the floor instead—one was filled with turnovers, the other with some cream. His thoughts and his eyes unconsciously fastened on these dainties. "Let us see," he said to himself, "how Patsyuk will eat the turnovers. He certainly won't want to bend down to lap them up like the dumplings; besides he couldn't—he must first dip the turnovers in the cream."

He had hardly time to think this when Patsyuk opened his mouth, looked at the turnovers, and opened his mouth wider still. At that moment a turnover popped out of the bowl, splashed into the cream, turned over on the other side, leaped upward, and flew straight into his mouth. Patsyuk ate it up and opened his mouth again, and another turnover went through the same performance. The only trouble he took was to munch it up and swallow it.

"My word, what a miracle!" thought the blacksmith, his mouth dropping open with surprise, and at the same moment he was aware that a turnover was creeping toward him and was already smearing his mouth with cream. Pushing away the turnover and wiping his lips, the blacksmith began to reflect what marvels there are in the world and to what subtle devices the evil spirit may lead a man, saying to himself at the same time that no one but Patsyuk could help him.

"I'll bow to him once more; maybe he will explain properly…. The devil, though! Why, today is a fast day and he is eating turnovers with meat in them! What a fool I am really. I am standing here and making ready to sin! Back …!" And the pious blacksmith ran headlong out of the cottage.

But the devil sitting in the sack and already gloating

over his prey could not endure to let such a glorious capture slip through his fingers. As soon as the blacksmith put down the sack the devil skipped out of it and mounted astride on his neck.

A cold shudder ran over the blacksmith's skin; pale and scared, he did not know what to do; he was on the point of crossing himself.... But the devil, putting his dog's nose down to Vakula's right ear, said: "It's I, your friend; I'll do anything for a friend and comrade! I'll give you as much money as you like," he squeaked into his left ear. "Oksana shall be yours this very day," he whispered, turning his nose again to the right ear. The blacksmith stood still, hesitating.

"Very well," he said at last; "for such a price I am ready to be yours!"

The devil clasped his hands in delight and began galloping up and down on the blacksmith's neck. "Now the blacksmith is done for!" he thought to himself: "now I'll pay you out, my dear, for all your paintings and false tales thrown up at the devils! What will my comrades say now when they learn that the most pious man of the whole village is in my hands!"

Here the devil laughed with joy, thinking how he would taunt all the long-tailed crew in hell, how furious the lame devil, who was considered the most resourceful among them, would be.

"Well, Vakula!" piped the devil, not dismounting from

his neck, as though afraid he might escape, "you know nothing is done without a contract."

"I am ready!" said the blacksmith. "I have heard that among you contracts are signed with blood. Stay, I'll get a nail out of my pocket!"

And he put his hand behind him and caught the devil by the tail.

"What a man you are for a joke!" cried the devil, laughing. "Come, let go, that's enough mischief!"

"Wait a bit, friend!" cried the blacksmith, "and what do you think of this?" As he said that he made the sign of the cross and the devil became as meek as a lamb. "Wait a bit," said the blacksmith, pulling him by the tail to the ground: "I'll teach you to entice good men and honest Christians into sin."

Here the blacksmith leaped astride on the devil and lifted his hand to make the sign of the cross.

"Have mercy, Vakula!" the devil moaned piteously; "I will do anything you want, anything; only let me off with my life: do not lay the terrible cross upon me!"

"Ah, so that's your note now, you damned German! Now I know what to do. Carry me at once on yourself! Do you hear? And fly like a bird!"

"Whither?" asked the miserable devil.

"To Petersburg, straight to the Tsaritsa!" And the blacksmith almost swooned with terror, as he felt himself mounting into the air.

* * *

Oksana stood for a long time pondering on the strange words of the blacksmith. Already an inner voice was telling her that she had treated him too cruelly. "What if he really does make up his mind to do something dreadful! I shouldn't wonder! Perhaps his sorrow will make him fall in love with another girl, and in his vexation he will begin calling her the greatest beauty in the village. But no, he loves me. I am so beautiful! He will not give me up for anything; he is playing, he is pretending. In ten minutes he will come back to look at me, for certain. I really was cross. I must, as though it were against my will, let him kiss me. Won't he be delighted!" And the frivolous beauty went back to jesting with her companions.

"Stay," said one of them, "the blacksmith has forgotten his sacks: look what terrible great sacks! He has made more by his carol-singing than we have. I fancy they must have put here quite a quarter of a sheep, and I am sure that there are no end of sausages and loaves in them. Glorious! we shall have enough to feast on for all Christmas week!"

"Are they the blacksmith's sacks?" asked Oksana. "We had better drag them to my cottage and have a good look at what he has put in them."

All the girls laughingly approved of this proposal.

"But we can't lift them!" the whole group cried, trying to move the sacks.

"Wait a minute," said Oksana; "let us run for a sledge and take them away on it!"

And the crowd of girls ran out to get a sledge.

The captives were dreadfully bored with staying in the sacks, although the sacristan had poked a fair-sized hole to peep through. If there had been no one about, he might have found a way to creep out; but to creep out of a sack before everybody, to be a laughingstock … that thought restrained him, and he made up his mind to wait, only uttering a slight groan under Tchub's ill-mannered boots.

Tchub himself was no less desirous of freedom, feeling that there was something under him that was terribly uncomfortable to sit upon. But as soon as he heard his daughter's plan, he felt relieved and did not want to creep out, reflecting that it must be at least a hundred paces and perhaps two hundred to his hut; if he crept out, he would have to set himself to rights, button up his sheepskin, fasten his belt—such a lot of trouble! Besides, his winter cap had been left at Soloha's. Let the girls drag him in the sledge.

But things turned out not at all as Tchub was expecting. Just when the girls were running to fetch the sledge, his lean neighbor, Panas, came out of the tavern, upset and ill-humored. The woman who kept the tavern could not be persuaded to serve him on credit. He thought to sit on in the tavern in the hope that some godly gentleman would come along and stand him treat; but as ill-luck would have it, all the gentlefolk were staying at home and like good Christians were eating rice and honey in the bosom of their families. Meditating on the degeneration of manners and the hard heart of the Jewess who kept the tavern, Panas made his way up to the sacks and stopped in amazement. "My word, what sacks somebody has flung down in the road!" he said, looking about him in all directions. "I'll be bound there is pork in them. Some carol-singer is in luck to get so many gifts of all sorts! What terrible great sacks! Suppose they are only stuffed full of buckwheat cake and biscuits, that's worth having; if there should be nothing but flat-cakes in them, that would be welcome, too; the Jewess would give me a dram of vodka for each cake. Let's make haste and get them away before anyone sees."

Here he flung on his shoulder the sack with Tchub and the sacristan in it, but felt it was too heavy. "No, it'll be too heavy for one to carry." he said; "and here by good luck comes the weaver Shapuvalenko. Good evening, Ostap!"

"Good evening!" said the weaver, stopping.

"Where are you going?"

"Oh, nowhere in particular."

"Help me carry these sacks, good man! Someone has been singing carols, and has dropped them in the middle of the road. We'll go halves over the things."

"Sacks? sacks of what? White loaves or flat-cakes?"

"Oh, all sorts of things, I expect."

They hurriedly pulled some sticks out of the fence, laid the sack on them, and carried it on their shoulders.

"Where shall we take it? To the tavern?" the weaver asked on the way.

"That's just what I was thinking; but, you know, the damned Jewess won't trust us, she'll think we have stolen it somewhere; besides, I have only just come from the tavern. We'll take it to my hut. No one will hinder us there, the wife's not at home."

"Are you sure she is not at home?" the prudent weaver inquired.

"Thank God that I am not quite a fool yet," said Panas; "the devil would hardly take me where she is. I expect she will be trailing round with the other women till daybreak."

"Who is there?" shouted Panas's wife, opening the door of the hut as she heard the noise in the porch made by the two friends with the sack. Panas was dumbfounded.

"Here's a go!" articulated the weaver, letting his hands fall.

Panas's wife was a treasure of a kind that is not uncommon in this world. Like her husband, she hardly ever stayed at home, but almost every day visited various cronies and well-to-do old women, flattered them, and ate with good appetite at their expense; she only quarreled with her husband in the mornings, as it was only then that she sometimes saw him. Their hut was twice as old as the district clerk's trousers; there was no straw in places on their thatched roof. Only the remnants of a fence could be seen, for everyone, as he went out of his house, thought it unnecessary to take a stick for the dogs, relying on passing by Panas's kitchen-garden and pulling one out of his fence.

The stove was not heated for three days at a time. Whatever the tender wife managed to beg from good Christians she hid as far as possible out of her husband's reach, and often wantonly robbed him of his gains if he had not had time to spend them on drink. In spite of his habitual imperturbability Panas did not like to give way to her, and consequently left his house every day with both eyes blackened, while his better half, sighing and groaning, waddled off to tell her old friends of her husband's unmannerliness and the blows she had to put up with from him.

Now you can imagine how disconcerted were the weaver and Panas by this unexpected apparition. Dropping the sack, they stood before it, and concealed it with their skirts, but it was already too late: Panas's wife, though she did not see well with her old eyes, had observed the sack.

"Well, that's good!" she said, with a face which betrayed the joy of a vulture. "That's good, that you have gained so much, singing carols! That's how it always is with good Christians; but no, I expect you have filched it somewhere. Show me your sack at once, do you hear, show me this very minute!"

"The bald devil may show you, but we won't," said Panas, assuming a dignified air.

"What's it to do with you?" said the weaver. "We've sung the carols, not you."

"Yes, you will show me, you wretched drunkard!" screamed the wife, striking her tall husband on the chin with her fist and forcing her way toward the sack. But the weaver and Panas manfully defended the sack and compelled her to beat a retreat. Before they recovered themselves the wife ran out again with an oven-fork in her hands. She nimbly caught her husband a thwack on the arms and the weaver one on his back and reached for the sack.

"Why did we let her pass?" said the weaver, coming to himself.

"Ay, we let her pass! Why did you let her pass?" said Panas coolly.

"Your oven-fork is made of iron, seemingly!" said the weaver after a brief silence, rubbing his back. "My wife bought one last year at the fair, gave twenty-five kopecks; that one's all right … it doesn't hurt…."

Meanwhile the triumphant wife, setting the potlamp on the floor, untied the sack and peeped into it.

But her old eyes, which had so well described the sack, this time certainly deceived her.

"Oh, but there is a whole pig lying here!" she shrieked, clapping her hands in glee.

"A pig! Do you hear, a whole pig!" The weaver nudged Panas. "And it's all your fault."

"It can't be helped!" replied Panas, shrugging his shoulders.

"Can't be helped! Why are we standing still? Let us take away the sack! Here, come on! Go away, go away. It's our pig!" shouted the weaver, stepping forward.

"Go along, go along, you devilish woman! It's not your property!" said Panas, approaching.

His wife picked up the oven-fork again, but at that moment Tchub crawled out of the sack and stood in the middle of the room, stretching like a man who has just woken up from a long sleep. Panas's wife shrieked, slapping her skirts, and they all stood with open mouths.

"Why did she say it was a pig, the silly! It's not a pig!" said Panas, gazing open-eyed.

"My word! What a man has been dropped into a sack!" said the weaver, staggering back in alarm. "You may say what you please, you can burst if you like, but the foul fiend has had a hand in it. Why, he would not go through a window!"

"It's Tchub!" cried Panas, looking more closely.

"Why, who did you think it was?" said Tchub, laughing. "Well, haven't I played you a fine trick? I'll be bound you meant to eat me by way of pork! Wait a bit, I'll console you: there is something in the sack; if not a whole pig, it's certainly a little porker or some live beast. Something was continually moving under me."

The weaver and Panas flew to the sack, the lady of the house clutched at the other side of it, and the battle would have been renewed had not the sacristan, seeing that now he had no chance of concealment, scrambled out of the sack of its own accord.

The woman, astounded, let go of the leg by which she

was beginning to drag the sacristan out of the sack.

"Here's another of them!" cried the weaver in horror, "the devil knows what has happened to the world…. My head's going round…. Men are put into sacks instead of cakes or sausages!"

"It's the sacristan!" said Tchub, more surprised than any of them. "Well, then! You're a nice one, Soloha! To put one in a sack…. I thought at the time her hut was very full of sacks…. Now I understand it all: she had a couple of men hidden in each sack. While I thought it was only me she … So there you have her!"

The girls were a little surprised on finding that one sack was missing.

"Well, there is nothing for it, we must be content with this one," murmured Oksana.

The mayor made up his mind to keep quiet, reasoning that if he called out to them to untie the sack and let him out, the silly girls would run away in all directions; they would think that the devil was in the sack—and he would be left in the street till next day. Meanwhile the girls, linking arms together, flew like a whirlwind with the sledge over the crunching snow. Many of them sat on the sledge for fun; others even clambered onto the top of the mayor. The mayor made up his mind to endure everything.

At last they arrived, threw open the door into the outer room of the hut, and dragged in the sack amid laughter.

"Let us see what is in it," they all cried, hastening to untie it.

At this point the hiccup which had tormented the mayor became so much worse that he began hiccuping and coughing loudly.

"Ah, there is someone in it!" they all shrieked, and rushed out of doors in horror.

"What the devil is it? Where are you tearing off to as though you were all possessed?" said Tchub, walking in at the door.

"Oh, daddy!" cried Oksana, "there is someone in the sack!"

"In the sack? Where did you get this sack?"

"The blacksmith threw it in the middle of the road," they all said at once.

"So that's it; didn't I say so?" Tchub thought to himself. "What are you frightened at? Let us look. Come now, my man—I beg you won't be offended at our not addressing you by your proper name—crawl out of the sack!"

The mayor did crawl out.

"Oh!" shrieked the girls.

"So the mayor got into one, too," Tchub thought to himself in bewilderment, scanning him from head to foot. "Well, I'm blessed!" He could say nothing more.

The mayor himself was no less confused and did not know how to begin. "I expect it is a cold night," he said, addressing Tchub.

"There is a bit of a frost," answered Tchub. "Allow me

to ask you what you rub your boots with, goose-fat or tar?" He had not meant to say that; he had meant to ask: "How did you get into that sack, mayor?" and he did not himself understand how he came to say something utterly different.

"Tar is better," said the mayor. "Well, good-night. Tchub!" and pulling his winter cap down over his head, he walked out of the hut.

"Why was I such a fool as to ask him what he rubbed his boots with?" said Tchub, looking toward the door by which the mayor had gone out.

"Well, Soloha is a fine one! To put a man like that in a sack …! My word, she is a devil of a woman! While I, poor fool … But where is that damned sack?"

"I flung it in the comer, there is nothing more in it," said Oksana.

"I know all about that; nothing in it, indeed! Give it here; there is another one in it! Shake it well…. What, nothing? My word, the cursed woman! And to look at her she is like a saint, as though she had never tasted anything but lenten fare …!"

But we will leave Tchub to pour out his vexation at leisure and will go back to the blacksmith, for it must be past eight o'clock.

At first it seemed dreadful to Vakula, particularly when he rose up from the earth to such a height that he could see nothing below, and flew like a fly so close under the moon that if he had not bent down he would have caught his cap in it. But in a little while he gained confidence and even began mocking the devil. (He was extremely amused by the way the devil sneezed and coughed when he took the little cyprus-wood cross off his neck and held it down to him. He purposely raised his hand to scratch his head, and the devil, thinking he was going to make the sign of the cross over him, flew along more swiftly than ever.) It was quite light at that height. The air was transparent, bathed in a light silvery mist. Everything was visible, and he could even see a wizard whisk by them like a hurricane, sitting in a pot, and the stars gathering together to play hide-and-seek, a whole swarm of spirits whirling away in a cloud, a devil dancing in the light of the moon and taking off his cap at the sight of the blacksmith galloping by, a broom flying back home, from which evidently a witch had just alighted at her destination…. And many other nasty things besides they met. They all stopped at the sight of the blacksmith to stare at him for a moment, and then whirled off and went on their way again. The blacksmith flew on till all at once Petersburg flashed before him, glittering with lights. (There happened to be an illumination that day.) The devil, flying over the city gate, turned into a horse and the blacksmith found himself mounted on a fiery steed in the middle of the street.

My goodness! the clatter, the uproar, the brilliant light; the walls rose up, four stories on each side; the thud of the horses' hooves and the rumble of the wheels echoed and resounded from every quarter; houses seemed to start up out of the ground at every step; the bridges trembled; carriages raced along; sledge-drivers and postilions shouted; the snow crunched under the thousand sledges flying from all parts; people passing along on foot huddled together, crowded under the houses which were studded with little lamps, and their immense shadows flitted over the walls with their heads reaching the roofs and the chimneys.

The blacksmith looked about him in amazement. It seemed to him as though all the houses had fixed their innumerable fiery eyes upon him, watching. Good Lord! he saw so many gentlemen in cloth fur-lined overcoats that he did not know whom to take off his cap to. "Good gracious, what a lot of gentry here!" thought the blacksmith. "I fancy everyone who comes along the street in a fur coat is the assessor and again the assessor! And those who are driving about in such wonderful chaises with glass windows, if they are not police-captains they certainly must be commissars or perhaps something grander still." His words were cut short by a question from the devil:

"Am I to go straight to the Tsaritsa?"

"No, I'm frightened," thought the blacksmith. "The Zaporozhtsy, who marched in the autumn through Dikanka, are stationed here, where I don't know. They came from the camp with papers for the Tsaritsa; anyway I might ask their advice. Hey, Satan! creep into my pocket and take me to the Zaporozhtsy!"

And in one minute the devil became so thin and small that he had no difficulty creeping into the blacksmith's pocket. And before Vakula had time to look round he found himself in front of a big house, went up a staircase, hardly knowing what he was doing, opened a door, and drew back a little from the brilliant light on seeing the smartly furnished room; but he regained confidence a little when he recognized the Cossacks who had ridden through Dikanka and now, sitting on silk-covered sofas, their tar-smeared boots tucked under them, were smoking the strongest tobacco, usually called "root."

"Good-day to you, gentlemen! God be with you, this is where we meet again," said the blacksmith, going up to them and swinging off a low bow.

"What man is that?" the one who was sitting just in front of the blacksmith asked another who was further away.

"You don't know me?" said the blacksmith. "It's I, Vakula, the blacksmith! When you rode through Dikanka in the autumn you stayed nearly two days with me. God give you all health and long years! And I put a new iron hoop on the front wheel of your chaise!"

"Oh!" said the same Cossack, "it's that blacksmith who paints so well. Good-day to you, neighbor! How has God brought you here?"

"Oh, I just wanted to have a look round. I was told …"

"Well, neighbor," said the Cossack, drawing himself up with dignity and wishing to show he could speak Russian too, "well, it's a big city."

The blacksmith, too, wanted to keep up his credit and not to seem like a novice. Moreover, as we have had occasion to see before, he too could speak like a book.

"A considerable town!" he answered carelessly. "There is no denying the houses are very large, the pictures that are hanging up are uncommonly good. Many of the houses are painted exuberantly with letters in gold leaf. The configuration is superb, there is no other word for it!"

The Zaporozhtsy, hearing the blacksmith express himself so freely, drew the most flattering conclusions in regard to him.

"We will have a little more talk with you, neighbor; now we are going at once to the Tsaritsa."

"To the Tsaritsa? Oh, be so kind, gentlemen, as to take me with you!"

"You?" a Cossack pronounced in the tone in which an old man speaks to his four-year-old charge when the latter asks to be seated on a real, big horse. "What would you do there? No, we can't do that. We are going to talk about our own affairs to the Tsaritsa." And his face assumed an expression of great significance.

"Do take me!" the blacksmith persisted.

"Ask them to!" he whispered softly to the devil, banging on the pocket with his fist.

He had hardly said this, when another Cossack brought out: "Do let us take him, mates!"

"Yes, do let us take him!" others joined in.

"Put on the same dress as we are wearing, then."

The blacksmith was hastily putting on a green tunic when all at once the door opened and a man covered with gold lace said it was time to go.

Again the blacksmith was moved to wonder, as he was whisked along in an immense coach swaying on springs, as four-storied houses raced by him on both sides and the rumbling pavement seemed to be moving under the horses' hooves.

"My goodness, how light it is!" thought the blacksmith to himself. "At home it is not so light as this in the daytime."

The coaches stopped in front of the palace. The Cossacks got out, went into a magnificent vestibule, and began ascending a brilliantly lighted staircase.

"What a staircase!" the blacksmith murmured to himself, "it's a pity to trample it with one's feet. What decorations! They say the stories tell lies! The devil a bit they do! My goodness! what banisters, what workmanship! Quite fifty roubles must have gone on the iron alone!"

When they had mounted the stairs, the Cossacks walked through the first drawing room. The blacksmith followed them timidly, afraid of slipping on the parquet at every footstep. They walked through three drawing rooms, the blacksmith still overwhelmed with admiration. On entering the fourth, he could not help going up to a picture hanging on the wall. It was the Holy Virgin with the Child in her arms.

"What a picture! What a wonderful painting!" he thought. "It seems to be speaking! It seems to be alive! And the Holy Child! It's pressing its little hands together and laughing, poor thing! And the colors! My goodness, what colors! I fancy there is not a kopeck-worth of ochre on it, it's all emerald green and crimson lake. And the blue simply glows! A fine piece of work! I expect the background was put in with the most expensive white lead. Wonderful as that painting is, though, this copper handle," he went on, going up to the door and fingering the lock, "is even more wonderful. Ah, what a fine finish! That's all done, I expect, by German blacksmiths and most expensive."

Perhaps the blacksmith would have gone on reflecting for a long time, if a flunkey in livery had not nudged his arm and reminded him not to lag behind the others. The Cossacks passed through two more rooms and then stopped. They were told to wait in the third, in which there was a group of several generals in gold-laced uniforms. The Cossacks bowed in all directions and stood all together.

A minute later, a rather thick-set man of majestic stature, wearing the uniform of a Hetman and yellow boots, walked in, accompanied by a regular suite. His hair was in disorder, he squinted a little, his face wore an expression of haughty dignity, and the habit of command could be seen in every movement. All the generals, who had been walking up and down rather superciliously in their gold uniforms, bustled about and seemed with low bows to be hanging on every word he uttered and even on his slightest gesture, so as to fly at once to carry out his wishes. But the Hetman did not even notice all that: he barely nodded to them and went up to the Cossacks.

The Cossacks all bowed down to the ground.

"Are you all here?" he asked deliberately, speaking a little through his nose.

"All, little father!" answered the Cossacks, bowing again.

"Don't forget to speak as I have told you!"

"No, little father, we will not forget."

"Is that the Tsar?" asked the blacksmith of one of the Cossacks.

"Tsar, indeed! It's Potemkin himself," answered the other.

Voices were heard in the other room, and the blacksmith did not know which way to look for the number of ladies who walked in, wearing satin gowns with long trains, and courtiers in gold-laced coats with their hair tied in a tail at the back. He could see a blur of brilliance and nothing more.

The Cossacks all bowed down at once to the floor and cried out with one voice: "Have mercy, little mother, mercy!"

The blacksmith, too, though seeing nothing, stretched himself very zealously on the floor.

"Get up!" An imperious and at the same time pleasant

voice sounded above them. Some of the courtiers bustled about and nudged the Cossacks.

"We will not get up, little mother! We will not get up! We will die, but we will not get up!" shouted the Cossacks.

Potemkin bit his lips. At last he went up himself and whispered peremptorily to one of the Cossacks. They rose to their feet.

Then the blacksmith, too, ventured to raise his head, and saw standing before him a short and, indeed, rather stout woman with blue eyes, and at the same time with that majestically smiling air which was so well able to subdue everything and could only belong to a queen.

"His Excellency has promised to make me acquainted today with my people whom I have not hitherto seen," said the lady with the blue eyes, scrutinizing the Cossacks with curiosity.

"Are you well cared for here?" she went on, going nearer to them.

"Thank you, little mother! The provisions they give us are excellent, though the mutton here is not at all like what we have in Zaporozhye ... What does our daily fare matter ...?"

Potemkin frowned, seeing that the Cossacks were saying something quite different from what he had taught them....

One of the Cossacks, drawing himself up with dignity, stepped forward:

"Be gracious, little mother! How have your faithful people angered you? Have we taken the hand of the vile Tatar?

Have we come to agreement with the Turk? Have we been false to you in deed or in thought? How have we lost your favor? First we heard that you were commanding fortresses to be built everywhere against us; then we heard you mean to turn us into carbineers; now we hear of new oppressions. Wherein are your Zaporozhye troops in fault? In having brought your army across the Perekop and helped your generals to slaughter the Tatars in the Crimea …?"

Potemkin casually rubbed with a little brush the diamonds with which his hands were studded and said nothing.

"What is it you want?" Catherine asked anxiously.

The Cossacks looked meaningly at one another.

"Now is the time! The Tsaritsa asks what we want!" the blacksmith said to himself, and he suddenly flopped down on the floor.

"Your Imperial Majesty, do not command me to be punished! Show me mercy! Of what, be it said without offense to your Imperial Graciousness, are the little slippers made that are on your feet? I fancy there is no Swede nor a shoemaker in any kingdom in the world can make them like that. Merciful heavens, if only my wife could wear slippers like that!"

The Empress laughed. The courtiers laughed too. Potemkin frowned and smiled both together. The Cossacks began nudging the blacksmith under the arm, wondering whether he had not gone out of his mind.

"Stand up!" the Empress said graciously. "If you wish to have slippers like these, it is very easy to arrange it. Bring him at once the very best slippers with gold on them! Indeed, this simple-heartedness greatly pleases me! Here you have a subject worthy of your witty pen!" the Empress went on, turning to a gentleman with a full but rather pale face, who stood a little apart from the others and whose modest coat with big mother-of-pearl buttons on it showed that he was not one of the courtiers.

"You are too gracious, your Imperial Majesty. It needs a La Fontaine at least to do justice to it!" answered the man with the mother-of-pearl buttons, bowing.

"I tell you sincerely, I have not yet got over my delight at your 'Brigadier.' You read so wonderfully well! I have heard, though," the Empress went on, turning again to the Cossacks, "that none of you are married in the Syetch."

"What next, little mother! Why, you know yourself, a man cannot live without a wife," answered the same Cossack who had talked to the blacksmith, and the blacksmith wondered, hearing him address the Tsaritsa as though purposely in coarse language, speaking like a peasant, as it is commonly called, though he could speak like a book.

"They are sly fellows!" he thought to himself. "I'll be bound he does not do that for nothing."

"We are not monks," the Cossack went on, "but sinful folk. Ready like all honest Christians to fall into sin. There are among us many who have wives, but do not live with them in the Syetch. There are some who have wives in Poland; there are some who have wives in Ukraine; there are some who have wives even in Turkey."

At that moment they brought the blacksmith the slippers.

"My goodness, what fine embroidery!" he cried joyfully, taking the slippers. "Your Imperial Majesty! If the slippers on your feet are like this—and in them Your Honor, I expect, goes sliding on the ice—what must the feet themselves be like! They must be made of pure sugar at least, I should think!"

The Empress, who had in fact very well-shaped and charming feet, could not help smiling at hearing such a compliment from the lips of a simple-hearted blacksmith, who in his Zaporozhets dress might be reckoned a handsome fellow in spite of his swarthy face.

Delighted with such gracious attention, the blacksmith would have liked to have cross-questioned the pretty Tsaritsa thoroughly about everything: whether it was true that tsars eat nothing but honey, fat bacon, and suchlike; but, feeling that the Cossacks were digging him in the ribs, he made up his mind to keep quiet. And when the Empress, turning to the older men, began questioning them about their manner of life and customs in the Syetch, he, stepping back, stooped down to his pocket and said softly: "Hurry me away from here and make haste!" And at once he found himself outside the city gates.

"He is drowned! On my word he is drowned! May I never leave this spot if he is not drowned!" lisped the weaver's fat wife, standing with a group of Dikanka women in the middle of the street.

"Why, am I a liar then? Have I stolen anyone's cow? Have I put the evil eye on someone, that I am not to be believed?" shouted a purple-nosed woman in a Cossack tunic, waving her arms. "May I never want to drink water again if old Dame Perepertchih didn't see with her own eyes the blacksmith hanging himself!"

"Has the blacksmith hanged himself? Well, I never!" said the mayor, coming out of Tchub's hut, and he stopped and pressed closer to the group.

"You had better say, may you never want to drink vodka, you old drunkard!" answered the weaver's wife. "He had need to be as mad as you to hang himself! He drowned himself! He drowned himself in the hole in the ice! I know that as well as I know that you were in the tavern just now."

"You disgrace! See what she throws up against me!" the woman with the purple nose retorted wrathfully. "You had better hold your tongue, you wretch! Do you think I don't know that the sacristan comes to see you every evening?"

The weaver's wife flared up.

"What about the sacristan? Whom does the sacristan go to? What lies are you telling?"

"The sacristan?" piped the sacristan's wife, squeezing her way up to the combatants, in an old blue cotton coat lined with hareskin. "I'll let the sacristan know! Who was it said the sacristan?"

"Well, this is the lady the sacristan visits!" said the woman with the purple nose, pointing to the weaver's wife.

"So it's you, you bitch!" said the sacristan's wife, stepping up to the weaver's wife. "So it's you, is it, witch, who cast a spell over him and gave him a foul poison to make him come to you!"

"Get thee behind me, Satan!" said the weaver's wife, staggering back.

"Oh, you cursed witch, may you never live to see your children! Wretched creature! Tfoo!"

Here the sacristan's wife spat straight into the other woman's face.

The weaver's wife endeavored to do the same, but spat instead on the unshaven chin of the mayor, who had come close up to the combatants that he might hear the quarrel better.

"Ah, nasty woman!" cried the mayor, wiping his face with the skirt of his coat and lifting his whip.

This gesture sent them all flying in different directions, scolding loudly.

"How disgusting!" repeated the mayor, still wiping his face. "So the blacksmith is drowned! My goodness! What a fine painter he was! What good knives and reaping-hooks and ploughs he could forge! What a strong man he was! Yes," he went on musing; "there are not many fellows like that in our village. To be sure, I did notice while I was in that damned sack that the poor fellow was very much depressed. So that is the end of the blacksmith! He was and is not! And I was meaning to have my dapple mare shod …!" And filled with such Christian reflections, the mayor quietly made his way to his own cottage.

Oksana was much troubled when the news reached her. She put little faith in Dame Perepertchih's having seen it and in the women's talk; she knew that the blacksmith was rather too pious a man to bring himself to send his soul to perdition. But what if he really had gone away, intending never to return to the village? And, indeed, in any place it would be hard to find as fine a fellow as the blacksmith. And how he loved her! He had borne with her caprices longer than any one of them.… All night long the beauty turned over from her right side to her left and her left to her right, and could not go to sleep. Now tossing in bewitching nakedness which the darkness concealed even from herself, she reviled herself almost aloud; now growing quieter, made up her mind to think of nothing—and kept thinking all the time. She was in a perfect fever, and by the morning head over ears in love with the blacksmith.

Tchub expressed neither pleasure nor sorrow at Vakula's fate. His thoughts were absorbed by one subject: he could not forget the treachery of Soloha and never left off abusing her even in his sleep.

Morning came. Even before daybreak the church was full of people. Elderly women in white linen wimples, in white cloth tunics, crossed themselves piously at the church porch. Ladies in green and yellow blouses, some even in dark blue overdresses with gold streamers behind, stood in front of them. Girls who had a whole shopful of ribbons twined on their heads, and necklaces, crosses, and coins round their necks, tried to make their way closer to the ikon-stand. But in front of all stood the gentlemen and humble peasants with mustaches, with forelocks, with thick necks and newly shaven chins, for the most part wearing hooded cloaks, below which peeped a white or sometimes a dark blue jacket. Wherever one looked, every face had a festive air. The mayor was licking his lips in anticipation of the sausage with which he would break his fast; the girls were thinking how they would slide with the lads on the ice; the old women murmured prayers more zealously than ever. All over the church one could hear the Cossack Sverbyguz bowing to the ground. Only Oksana stood feeling unlike herself: she prayed without praying. So many different feelings, each more amazing, each more distressing than the other, crowded upon her heart that her face expressed nothing but overwhelming confusion; tears quivered in her eyes. The girls could not think why it was and did not suspect that the blacksmith was responsible. However, not only Oksana was concerned about the blacksmith. All the villagers observed that the holiday did not seem like a holiday, that something was lacking. To make things worse, the sacristan was hoarse after his travels in the sack and he wheezed scarcely audibly; it is true that the chorister who was on a visit to the village sang the bass splendidly, but how much better it would have been if they had had the blacksmith too, who used always when they were singing *Our Father* or the *Holy Cherubim* to step up into the choir and from there sing it with the same chant with which it is sung in Poltava. Moreover, he alone performed the duty of a churchwarden. Matins were already over; after matins mass was over.... Where indeed could the blacksmith have vanished to?

It was still night as the devil flew even more swiftly back with the blacksmith, and in a trice Vakula found himself inside his own cottage. At that moment the cock crowed.

"Where are you off to?" cried the blacksmith, catching the devil by his tail as he was about to run away. "Wait a bit, friend, that's not all: I haven't thanked you yet." Then, seizing a switch, he gave him three lashes and the poor devil set to running like a peasant who has just had a hiding from the tax-assessor. And so, instead of tricking, tempting, and fooling others, the enemy of mankind was fooled himself. After that Vakula went into the outer room, made himself a hole in the hay, and slept till dinnertime. When he woke up he was frightened at seeing that the sun was already high, "I've overslept myself and missed matins and mass!"

Then the worthy blacksmith was overwhelmed with distress, thinking that no doubt God, as a punishment for his sinful intention of damning his soul, had sent this heavy sleep, which had prevented him from even being in church on this solemn holiday. However, comforting himself with the thought that next week he would confess all this to the priest and that from that day he would begin making fifty bows a day for a whole year, he glanced into the cottage; but there was no one there. Apparently Soloha had not yet returned.

Carefully he drew out from the breast of his coat the slippers and again marveled at the costly workmanship and the wonderful adventure of the previous night. He washed and dressed himself in his best, put on the very clothes which he had got from the Cossacks, took out of a chest a new cap of good astrakhan with a dark blue top not once worn since he had bought it while staying in Poltava; he also took out a new girdle of rainbow colors; he put all this together with a whip in a kerchief and set off straight to see Tchub.

Tchub opened his eyes wide when the blacksmith walked into his cottage, and did not know what to wonder at most: the blacksmith's having risen from the dead, the blacksmith's having dared to come to see him, or the blacksmith's being dressed up such a dandy, like a Zaporozhets. But he was even more astonished when Vakula untied the kerchief and laid before him a new cap and a girdle such as had never been seen in the village, and then plumped down on his knees before him, and said in a tone of entreaty: "Have mercy, father! Be not wroth! Here is a whip; beat me as much as your heart may desire. I give myself up, I repent of everything! Beat, but only be not wroth. You were once a comrade of my father's, you ate bread and salt together and drank the cup of goodwill."

It was not without secret satisfaction that Tchub saw the blacksmith, who had never knocked under to anyone in the village and who could twist five-kopeck pieces and horseshoes in his hands like pancakes, lying now at his feet. In order to keep up his dignity still further, Tchub took the whip and gave him three strokes on the back. "Well, that's enough; get up! Always obey the old! Let us forget everything that has passed between us. Come, tell me now what is it that you want?"

"Give me Oksana to wife, father!"

Tchub thought a little, looked at the cap and the girdle. The cap was delightful and the girdle, too, was not inferior to it; he thought of the treacherous Soloha and said resolutely: "Good! send the matchmakers!"

"Aïe!" shrieked Oksana, as she crossed the threshold and saw the blacksmith, and she gazed at him with astonishment and delight.

"Look, what slippers I have brought you!" said Vakula, "they are the same as the Tsaritsa wears!"

"No, no! I don't want slippers!" she said, waving her

arms and keeping her eyes fixed upon him, "I am ready without slippers...." She blushed and could say no more.

The blacksmith went up to her and took her by the hand; the beauty looked down. Never before had she looked so exquisitely lovely. The enchanted blacksmith gently kissed her; her face flushed crimson and she was even lovelier still.

The bishop of blessed memory was driving through Dikanka. He admired the site on which the village stands, and as he drove down the street stopped before a new cottage.

"And whose is this cottage so gaily painted?" asked His Reverence of a beautiful woman, who was standing near the door with a baby in her arms.

"The blacksmith Vakula's!" Oksana, for it was she, told him, bowing.

"Splendid! splendid work!" said His Reverence, examining the doors and windows. The windows were all outlined with a ring of red paint; everywhere on the doors there were Cossacks on horseback with pipes in their teeth.

But His Reverence was even warmer in his praise of Vakula when he learned that by way of church penance he had painted free of charge the whole of the left choir green with red flowers.

But that was not all. On the wall, to one side as you go in at the church, Vakula had painted the devil in hell—such a loathsome figure that everyone spat as he passed. And the women would take a child up to the picture, if it would go on crying in their arms, and would say: "There, look! What a caca!"* And the child, restraining its tears, would steal a glance at the picture and nestle closer to its mother.

*In Russian: "*Yaka kaka!*"— (*Ed.*)

Nikolai Gogol

"Gogol was a strange creature, but genius is always strange."
—Vladimir Nabokov

Nikolai Gogol (1809–1852) was born in Ukraine. His first story collection, *Evenings on a Farm near Dikanka*, was based on Ukrainian themes and was a great success. After completing *The Government Inspector*, a satirical masterpiece mocking Russian bureaucracy, Gogol traveled throughout Europe, where he wrote his greatest prose works, the novel *Dead Souls* and the stories "The Overcoat," "The Nose," and "Diary of a Madman." On his return to Russia, he became depressed and repeatedly burned his manuscripts. Under the influence of a church elder, he burned the second and third parts of *Dead Souls* for the final time, then took to his bed and refused to eat. He died of starvation nine days later.

Constance Garnett (1861–1946) learned Russian while at Cambridge. After a visit to Russia during which she met Tolstoy, she was inspired to translate his work and that of Gogol, Dostoevsky, Turgenev, and Chekhov, among others. Her translations are met with great acclaim and remain highly influential.